Bringing
The Water Hyacinth
To Africa

for John

EVANGELINE PATERSON

Bringing The Water Hyacinth To Africa

TAXVS 1983

ACKNOWLEDGEMENTS

A number of these poems were previously collected in:

The Sky is Deep Enough (Starglow Press, 1972)
18 Poems (Outposts Publications, 1974)
Whitelight (Mid-Day Publications, Oxford, 1978)
Reprints (Other Poetry Editions, 1978, 1982)

Some were first printed in:

Anglo-Welsh Review, Anthology of Magazine Verse (USA), *Envoi, Gallery, Midlands Poetry Worksheet, New England Review* (USA), *New Poetry 9: An Arts Council Anthology, Other Poetry, Pequod* (USA), and *Poetry Durham*.

Copyright © Evangeline Paterson 1972, 1974, 1978, 1982, 1983
All rights reserved

ISBN: 1 85019 006 2

First published 1983 by

Taxvs Press,
30 Logan Street,
Langley Park,
Durham DH7 9YN.

Set in 11 on 12pt Chelmsford and printed by
Wards (Colour Printers) Dunston Tyne & Wear
Tel. 0632 605915

CONTENTS

Wife to Husband	9
Crazy Girl	10
Ballad of Marjorie	11
Miss Emily in White	12
Song for a Wandering Child	13
Gunna's Tale	14
Whitelight	15
Poem for Putzi Hanfstaengel	16
Death on a Crossing	17
lost season	18
Marseillaise	19
Room with Sea-Coloured Curtains	20
Parting from my Son	21
Advice to Daughters	22
The Betrayed Girl	23
Imelda's Mam	24
Jehanne	25
Poem for Langston Hughes	26
moon	27
A Moral Tale	28
Old Woman in the City	29
hard winter	30
History Teacher in the Warsaw Ghetto Rising	31
sometimes at morning	32
armaments race	33
Visitation	34
attic dweller	35
Ophelia's Ghost to Hamlet	36
Tribal Homeland	37
Bringing the Water Hyacinth to Africa	38
Dispossessed	39
In a South African Museum	40
Last night we put the clocks back	41
very early	42
Bad Day in January	43
Programme Note	44
Siesta	45
Triangle, with Camel	46
Leftright	47

A Haunting	48
Evening at Linderhof	49
between	50
Civilisation	51
Friend of the Family	52
Variations on a Street Song	53
Mrs. Pintrap	54
Old Wives' Tales	55
Herald of Spring	56
Camel Bells	57
Coming Alive	58
Apparition in W. H. Smith's	59
Instructions for a Funeral	60
Schoolgirls Crossing the Park	61

Wife to Husband

you are a person
like a tree
standing like rock
moving like water

you show me how
to hold like a root
and how to dance
in a changing rhythm

you hold me close
in a singing stillness
you rock me slow
in a crazy wind

you show me a height
that I may grow to
you cover the sky
with stars and branches

you lose your leaves
without complaining
you know there will be
another spring

you stand like rock
you move like water
you are a person
like a tree

Crazy Girl

I know a year in time when time stopped.
Now it runs backwards. No one has noticed yet.

But what I want to know is:
How did the elms know? And who told them?

I think of the dead, who went to their quiet graves
in the quiet earth, thinking the earth was a refuge.

I am afraid of the tree blossoming out of season,
and when the owl speaks in the dark I am afraid.

Ballad of Marjorie

McGill was hanged for lifting sheep,
And dangled from a chain,
A blackened thing that turned and turned
Beneath the wind and rain.

And Marjorie, who thought his step
Waked all her world to light,
And paused to hear him pass the lane
At morning and at night,

Could not endure that he whose look
Had lit her world with grace
Turned on a gibbet round and round
While ravens pecked his face.

An honest girl, as well she knew,
Could never love a thief,
And while she held her face like stone
All cankered grew her grief.

A thief, she knew, deserved to die,
But always in her brain
A twisted thing turned round, turned round
Upon a creaking chain.

She could not bear to hear the wind
Or walk beneath the sky,
Or see the faces of the folk
Who'd stood to watch him die.

Poor simple girl, she could not turn
Her stubborn heart by will,
And so she went to find the dark
Beneath a forest pool.

>   And who – the neighbours, parson, judge,
>   The hangman, or McGill –
>   Shall stand to answer for the death
>   Of Marjorie the fool?

Miss Emily in White

> '. . . Tom came in, and I ran
> to his Blue Jacket'
>   – Emily Dickinson –

Miss Emily in white
hoisted her flag
against death, knew him,
at last, as enemy.

Eroded
by losses, she withdrew
to her own ground, flashed signals
to immortality,
sent flowers, as emissaries,
to allies.

The day when the telegram came –
to say that Judge Lord was stricken –
there, in the front hall,
was Thomas Kelley, manservant,
bluff, familiar, kindly,
his rough blue jacket
to be clung to, cried on.

No need to weep for her.
She did well
in the war none can win

and had Thomas Kelley to hold to
when the first bastion fell.

Song for a Wandering Child

You fit in my heart
like a snail in its shell

when you are gone
the wind pours through me
the light drowns me

come home, I will wrap you
around and around
in the house I have made you
the wind shall not find you

light as a leaf
hollow as weed-stem
I echo with fears

come home, I will keep you
as safe as I may
from bird-beak and stone

Gunna's Tale

Three men came striding up from the shore,
Ranald, Wrybeard, and Wulf the Tall.
They rattled their knife-hilts on the door
And crowded in to my father's hall.

Wulf had a slow and sleepy eye.
Wrybeard's look was smouldering hot.
Ranald turned to look at the sky
And the back of his head was all I got.

They diced for me, as they drank, that night,
While my father sat by the fire and slept.
They woke me up in the first grey light,
And who would have listened, if I'd wept?

Wrybeard took me home to his hall.
Wrybeard took me in to his bed.
I bit my lip and stared at the wall
And counted the years till I could be dead.

Five sons I bore him – as any wife should –
Sullen, and heavy of brow, and black.
I mended their clothes and I cooked their food
Till they went their ways and never looked back.

And then, as I sat by the fire one night,
The sea rose up in a sudden squall.
They lay on the shore in the morning light,
Ranald, and Wrybeard, and Wulf the Tall.

I made a grave, and I sewed a pall,
One man long, and two men wide.
I buried Wrybeard and Wulf the Tall

And I thrust Ranald back in the tide.

Whitelight

Sunlight
loved her.   It
hummed in her veins.   She
filled her skin like an orange.

Owl-light
enhanced her.   Shadow
was a coat she could wear.

Starlight
compelled her.   Frost,
at her finger-ends, tingled.

Night
never dismayed her.
Her treasures glowed
in the dark.

       But when the flat white
       snow lay on every
       hedge, tree and bush
       that was a light
       that did not love her

       that showed her how
       she would look when she
       was old.

Poem for Putzi Hanfstaengel

> *Putzi Hanfstaengel, pianist, wit and bon viveur, was a permanent fixture in Hitler's entourage. The Fuhrer relied on Hanfstaengel's urbane presence to disarm visitors from the outside world. Through sheer exercise of his charm, he survived Hitler's increasing disenchantment with him, and escaped to America, where he lived to a respected old age.*

Clowning on the margin
of history's pages,
playing the piano for
your very good friend,
clever man, fun man,
nice-to-have-around man,
    oh Putzi Hanfstaengel,
    play for us again!

The ride you went along for
ended on the rapids.
You bobbed like a cork and
you floated again.
Now, on the telly-screen,
soft-spoken, charming,
    oh Putzi Hanfstaengel,
    play for us again!

Play it for us, like you
played it for Adolf,
and when it's time to go, boy,
you'd better play it then!
Outside the door six
million ghosts are waiting.
    Oh Putzi Hanfstaengel,
    clever Putzi Hanfstaengel,
    fun Putzi Hanfstaengel,
    better swing it then!

Death on a Crossing

What he never thought to consider was whether
the thing was true. What bewildered him, mostly,
was the way the rumours had of reaching him
from such improbable sources – illiterate pamphlets
pressed in his hand, the brash or the floundering stranger
who came to his door, the proclamations, among
so many others, on hoardings

                        though sometimes waking
a brief dismay, that never quite prodded him
to the analyst's couch.

                  But annunciations, he thought,
should come to a rational man in a rational way.
He walked between a skyful of midnight angels
and a patch on somebody's jeans, both saying
the same thing to his stopped ears

                            till the day
when he stepped on a crossing with not enough conviction
to get him safe to the other side, and he lay
among strangers' feet, and the angels lowered their trumpets
and no sweet chariot swung, to carry him home.

lost season

        there was not enough music
that spring, and the trees rocked in a
huddle of grief over their curled leaves

        and there was a whisper of crying
under the dumb sky, an echo of
steps going another way, a sound of
nobody coming

        and there was never enough
singing to lift the hyacinth heads, to loosen
the gnarled strings of winter, to let the leaves
uncurl their numb fingers under the sky

Marseillaise

When Marie-Louise was chopping the vegetables
in the kitchen of Madame Dupuy,
wife of the notary, in the city of Marseilles,
the sun shone and she sang,

not knowing that Jean-Paul Gautier
had been stabbed on the dockside that morning,
not even in his own quarrel,
he having a kind heart and not knowing
how to stay out of trouble,

and for Marie-Louise, being
a woman of limited intellect
and no independence of spirit,

the light went out in the kitchen of Madame Dupuy,
and over the streets and the harbour of Marseilles,
and over Europe and over Africa.

Room with Sea-Coloured Curtains

Half-waking early
before dawn, we move
closer, we lie twined,
half-sleeping still.

Blue and purple and green
gleam in our deep-sea chamber.
The rocking of many tides
has brought us here. The dull
weight of the years to come
moves like the tide above us.
We lie, like two halves
of a whole, in one shell.

The light will break soon
on the fanged rocks. The sea-birds
will wake us.

But this moment we hold
against all comers.

Parting from my Son

The plane wheels lurch, leave
the tarmac, tightening
the inescapable cord.
                        The tug
brings sudden tears. No use to call myself
a fool. Time has no help for
what ails me.

Son, grown to a colossus, striding
the streets in your high boots, spinning
your gaudy fantasies,
your desperado moustache is
no disguise to me.

I leave you where the wind
blows cold off the river

your dreams are not enough
to keep me warm.

Advice to Daughters

Beware the men who seek
the soft and changing tone
of youth upon the cheek
and overlook the bleak
white armature of bone.

He is a fool who loves
only the dimpled face.
It is in the bone that moves
ungainly, or with grace
to fill a singing space.

And time will come and hone
his sharp and eager beak
upon the flesh alone,
and then the bone will speak.

The Betrayed Girl

My name is Ha-no-mi.   I have chosen water.

Love that I met in the forest
ate me like a tiger.

Love that warmed my house
crackled like fire and spat me out.

In the black furrows I have borne my child,
my pure miracle, my heartbeat.
The world is not to be trusted with this.

Earth will not open.
Air is empty and whines like a ghost.
Fire cannot follow me. I turn towards water.

It will gulp once and swallow, then let us lie
curled together, closer than breathing.
It will finger our eyelids, singing of sleep.

My name is Ha-no-mi.   I have chosen water.

Imelda's Mam

That was the first time when it come to me
what a queer thing is death, when Imelda's mam
was being let down carefully into the ground,
everyone holding their breaths, her kin standing
solid and black in the cold, like trees, when Imelda,
twelve years old and spoiled rotten, screamed,
sharp as a stone through glass.
                                         I looked quick
at the coffin. I'm sure I don't know what I thought
I was going to see. Imelda's mam was always
one to come running half the width of the world
if Imelda skinned her knee. But nothing ever
lay so dark and quiet as that deep hole
she'd gone down into.
                             That's when it come to me
what a queer thing is death, what a mercy for some.

Jehanne

They say the men from the north are coming closer,
swallowing farms and villages as a hound
swallows gobbets. The monks are burying books
and gold vessels. The scholars and singers are gone
south. Only the holy anchorites,
whose piety is as savage as the northmen,
do not care what tide washes over them.

And I, Jehanne, in this orchard bury,
in many wrappings, as if it were a child,
the coverlet that I worked for five years of winters.
My lady said, Jehanne, when it is done
you will be ready for marriage. And this spring
she said, Jehanne, it is nearly done. Who
will you take beneath your coverlet? But none
is left now to come walking in the orchard
while I sit pricking love-knots with my needle.

So here, with no one watching, I lay the violets
and the coloured birds and the tall branching lilies.
If it please the saints I shall live, and have a daughter,
and teach her to make violets with a needle.
But who can tell? The dark is coming closer.

Poem for Langston Hughes

turning words over
fitting sorrows to sounds
I thought about Langston Hughes
who said 'They suffer in monosyllables
in Kansas'.

I never met you, Langston Hughes,
and there's nothing we can
tell each other now,

but you wrote this song down,
left it for me to find:
> *'Say, is you ever seen a*
> *one-eyed woman cry?'*

moon

lights flicker out
streets drain homeward
dark pours down

moon moves closer
wind hushes
teeth of frost glisten

moon moulds my face
like a mask, scoops
hollows for eyes

strokes
thin skin of my wrist
between sleeve and glove
hungers for bone

in this quaking hour
blood dwindles
pulse falters

moon speaks to bone
and bone answers

A Moral Tale

See young Mr. Parsons, down on a day excursion,
boatered and blazered, goatfoot along the pier,
spun like a top by the crowds, stunned by the sun,
stung with love like a gadfly, looking for Flora.

See Flora Wickerley, plump and easy laugher,
safely behind the ice cream parlour window
with her friend Aurelia, eating two flavours at once,
licking her spoon and laughing at Mr. Parsons.

See Flora, ten years older, a scream, a caution,
ever such fun, how old do you think she is? –
patrolling the promenade, the pier and the palais,
her eyes come-hithering and her feet aching.

See Mr. Parsons, balder, stouter, wiser,
safely stowed beside his slumbering spouse,
starting awake, in a hideous dream of Flora
holding his heart, like a winkle, on a pin.

Old Woman in the City

In carpet slippers she sluffs
along the cracked pavement, over the road
to the bench where she sits, muttering
and shunned. Flower stalls blaze
at her elbow. Pigeons flutter and strut
at her feet. She sits in her own dark, clutches
her everything in a paper bag.   Sullenness
shuts her in.

But I saw her once, in a phone booth,
furious, shouting into the dumb receiver:
'You got no respect for a person!
You got no respect!' – and stand
for a long time, listening,
under the notice saying 'Out of Order.'

hard winter

trees
do not forget
a starving winter

in shrill dawns
when birds rehearse
their creaking notes

and small shrubs gossip
busy with blossom

they stand stark
against the sky still

the winds will tease
new leaves to a flutter
                         but not
the ache from the wood nor the dark
ring from the core

where the bright axe will discover
to the woodman's eye that this
was a starving winter

History Teacher
in the Warsaw Ghetto Rising

after an engraving by
Maurice Mendjisky

The schoolmaster once known as
Umbrella Feet
unfolds his six-foot length
of gangling bone

and, mild as usual,
blinks – his bi-focals
having gone the way of his pipe
and his tree-shaded study
and his wife Charlotte –

and, jacket flapping, as usual,
carpet slippers treading
rubble of smashed cellars,

advancing steadily into the
glare of the burning street

and holding his rifle uncertainly
as if he thought it irrelevant
– as indeed it is –

he leads his scattered handful
of scarecrow twelve-year-olds

towards the last twenty minutes
of their own brief history.

sometimes at morning

      lay under a weight of dark heavy as water
      dreaming of eating honey with a spoon

in their cold nests the birds
stared all night long with jewelled eyes at nothing
unmoved by rumours of dawn

till day climbed up, hand over hand, clinging
with fingers of light to the sky's rim

      came up slowly
      dreaming of honey still

armaments race

and Mrs. Stephanopoulos said oh yes I am happy
I am very happy and why not for I have
a fine husband and beautiful children

and we have our health and enough to eat and we all
love each other exceedingly and If I had just one wish
this is what it would be

that when we die we should all go to heaven together
in the same instant so that none might feel
pain or despair at the losing of any other

and I said oh Mrs. Stephanopoulos oh my dear
you should be truly a happy woman for never
have so many been toiling with such a blinkered devotion
in the deep-down mines and the shiny laboratories
to make your one wish come true

Visitation

'Have you heard of angels?' said the visiting lady
to the little poor child. 'They have you in their keeping.
They hover around you when your prayers are said.
They whisper dreams in your ear when you are sleeping.'

Said the little poor child, 'I have seen them, tall as gantries
and thick as rain in the air above the town.
They all leaned one way like a field of wheat.
Their faces were white as paper. Their tears fell down.'

attic dweller

in a town of echoing streets and high gables
she lived between sky and sky
told time by birds passing

ching went the gold clock on her crooked stair
tick tock tick tock went her mind
clong went the tongue in the iron tower

clouds peered and jostled at her casement
winds lapped at her sill
her timbers creaked in all weathers

click click she netted her days with a bright needle
leaned out to trawl for stars

Ophelia's Ghost to Hamlet

If the owl is a baker's daughter
what, then, are you?
No, I'll not get me to a nunnery

nor trail in soaked skirts across your sky.
That is not what I see in this mirror.

I was keeled and tarred, seaworthy, urgent
for voyaging. You should have boarded me.

We would have skimmed a sea of troubles,
but when your voices waked us, then we drowned.

Truth is deep as a well. You have to go
a cold way down to find it.

Look where the moon peers, wheyface. Gape you at it.
You will not find your image in my eye.

Tribal Homeland

Here is the world's bitter end. Wind
is always blowing. Small mud houses cling
to the ground, their tin roofs weighted with stones.

Earth is trampled, here,
hard as brick. The bleak eroded hill
looks down, offers no hope, deflects no weather.

Across the waste comes a woman walking, flat
feet on cracked earth, blanket blazing orange-
yellow, bright as anger, loud as a bugle

under the threatening sky.
Now all sad music lapses out of key.
Something here is not going to die.

Bringing the Water Hyacinth to Africa

Planted in Africa, it floated
rafts of flowers on the wide
coils of the Congo, spread
hungry as flame over stream and tributary,

launched to the sea its unhurrying
blue-eyed flotillas, clogging
a continent's arteries, slowing
the march of progress to a crawl.

And who's to blame? Some say a priest
homesick for Florida, some say
a Belgian lady, all Africa
for her back yard, set out

to prettify the Congo.
And who's to say? But pity
whoever it was, who meant
no harm at all, and left, as monument

a thousand miles of curses and jammed propellers.

Dispossessed

This man is called Obed. His surname
is in another language. You do not need
to know it.

This is his room. He lives here
by himself. He does not have
enough food.

These are his wife and children.
They live a long way off. He sends them money.
They do not have enough food.

He goes home once a year. They run to meet him.
Sometimes they cry, we are told, from happiness.

He comes back to his room in the city,
where they are not allowed. They stay
in the hard land where nothing grows.

Does this discourage him? Who knows? He throws
no bombs. He breaks no windows.
He sends home money.

                    All his enterprise
is not forgetting.

In a South African Museum

The bushwoman lies
in a foetal crouch.
Her agile bones
hold no secrets.

Earth, shred by shred,
dismantled her. Wind,
whisper by whisper,
picked her clean.

The lady from Egypt lies
cocooned in cerements,
sealed blind and dumb, lacquered
with half a man's ransom
in peeling gold.
Her nose crumbles.

They lie, side by side,
awaiting the resurrection.

The lady moans.
No one can hear her.

The bushwoman grins.

Last night we put the clocks back.   Now

I lie awake in a cold dawn
with an hour more for grieving,

remembering
how once you would come, small apparition
troubled by dreams, to burrow into my arms,
and we would sleep, like one person
again.

It would ease me now to go
upstairs to where you lie
breathing lightly,
slip in beside you and
fall asleep. But no use
pretending,

and I will put no clock back
though mine creeps on to winter
and your case stands packed in the hall

and I lie in a cold dawn,
trickling tears on to a damp pillow,
calling myself names.

very early

for Seamus Heaney

this bird who wakes me
clear and early

stabbing sleep
to tell what happened

is saying it right
is saying it true

this I am not
too stupid to know

he says it twice
he says it precisely

stupid   thickfingered
I miss it again

Bad Day in January

today began with no kissing
and went to worse

              to opening
curtains late on shivering
twigs of laburnum waiting
for bad news in a splat of rain

              to coaxing
backyard birds by scattering
crumbs   but all away and declaiming
somewhere else

              to chafing
of chores against the complaining
reluctant grain

              to looking and looking
through rain-vexed panes for you coming
to start again with kissing

Programme Note

Seated on benches in the village hall,
we scan the duplicated sheet, listing
a queen or two, sundry lords and ladies,
assorted servitors. And the musicians,
the stage crew, the Mistress of the Wardrobe.

Then – afterthought, it seems – 'Bryony Adams,
box office, flute music and seagull noises'.

Let us applaud
this humble handmaid of the arts, through whom
the wayward muses speak with various voices.

The fates dispense their gifts in different sizes.
They also serve who make the seagull noises.

Siesta

The widows are all asleep
in the tall houses that frown across the green,
shutting the sun out. They lie in mounds
and billows of pillow and eiderdown. Their spouses
sleep too, but deeper and farther down.
In the dim rooms below
the maids move in the curtained gloom, preparing
the finicking meals for one, and the three cats
perhaps, or the two pekes, upholstered like bolsters.
They talk to themselves, laying the silver straight.

Sunk in sleep, the widows are tugging
loose, and light as girls again go floating
out and away, over the green, rapping
on headstones, 'Sam! Bert! George! Are you coming?
Children! Samantha, Edgar, Jason, come!'
Then off, down the path to the blackberry hedge,
the weedy pond, the leaning chestnut,
the knee-deep meadow buzzing with sun,

and Edgar, Samantha, Jason,
bejowled behind a desk, or befurred in a taxi,
nod in the drowsy afternoon, escape
to daisy chains in a knee-deep meadow.

Grappled at last by the hook
of the striking clock, the widows surface, rise,
go creaking and corseted down the wavering stair.
Sam, Bert, George turn over and sleep again.

Triangle, with Camel

The text beneath the photograph is brief,
merely 'Queen Elena leading a camel'.

There is nothing in the picture
but sea, sand, scrub, and Queen Elena
holding the camel's rope. She looks resigned.
The camel sneers like a Shakespearean actor.
Why is she leading it into the sea?

Over the page her spouse, Vittorio Emanuele,
baggy-trousered, diminutive, is leading
a furbelowed, black-browed beauty, whose name,
we are told, is La Bella Rosina. She seems calm
in spite of his furze-bush whiskers, boot-button eyes.

Has it occurred to the Queen
to leave La Bella Rosina holding the camel
and lead Vittorio Emanuele into the sea?

Leftright

In the year 1870
the Grand Duchy of Lichtenstein
sent eighty men
(leftright leftright
in their long overcoats)
and one cannon
to the Franco-Prussian War

and when the war was over
welcomed home again
(leftright leftright)
eightyone men
and one cannon

no one has ever
accounted for this

A Haunting

for Mahendra Solanki

That was a good story –
the old kimono'd woman
who shuffled each day to the corner
with a full packet of Daz
and at six o'clock precisely
emptied it down the drain.
When asked why, said only,
'Somebody's got to feed them.'

Now, walking home in winter
past gratings, I shudder
and look away, imagining
a dumb and endless waiting,
or wake, on troubled midnights,
wondering why we laughed,
thinking, beyond all reason,
'Nobody feeds them now.'

Evening at Linderhof

for Paul Bentley

Ludwig the king, beautiful once, and young,
broods on the balcony. His glance falls,
like dusk descending, over
crested hills whose peaks and pinnacles blossom
into his carved white fantasies of stone.

                      The towering fountain
rears, immense as his dream, lapses, thrusts
upward again to indigo pricked with gold.
Other men's dreams creep underground, turn wheels,
grind corn. His are harnessed to stars.

He turns – and the world with him – towards the dim
magnificent corridors. Shades of dead emperors
wait to be summoned. Music attends him.

                      What splinter of light
refracts from mirrors, distracts him?

                      Turning aside,
he takes up a pen, and writes:
'Remind me to look happier tomorrow.'

between

there is always time to think
while the tap runs and the water fills the sink

who knows what might waken,
while watching the eggs, while turning over the bacon

between one June and another June
a year can pass like a sleepy afternoon

yet there is time for epiphanies between
ironing the blue pyjamas and the green

Civilisation

Saturday afternoon. Professor Paterson
walks in his garden, bends on his daffodils
looks fond yet stern. His brain, unoccupied, idles.
He hums. Half-heartedly, the watery sun
attempts to gild him, like a saint. He moves
away, deeply ponders a hole in the fence,
reproves a dangling creeper.

                          His wife, in the kitchen,
scours the pans. The radio chatters calamity.
Civilisation is teetering to a fall.
Music erupts, with thud and boom and crash
– the mangonels of the last assault? She sluices
water around the sink. She drops a cup.
It shatters.

                        Professor Paterson
sits in his usual chair, and reads. Daffodils
stand in a vase behind him. He looks kindly
over his spectacles. The world settles
back on its base.

                    Civilisation, it seems,
is with us yet. She goes to make him tea.

Friend of the Family

One sees at a glance that you are the Bad Companion,
a-dazzle with charm, a-glitter with savoir faire.

When the innocent hero steps out into life's morning,
fresh from the admonitions of his mother
and the tears of his nurse, who lies in wait but you?

And then the expensive gaming club, the brandy,
the ashen face and a pistol the morning after –

or else the letter home, and the squalid voyage
incognito to the farthest Antipodes,
the years away, the return to scenes of childhood –

only to find you'd got to his favourite sister,
beguiled her away from her husband, the worthy vicar,
and left her to starve in an attic in Florence –

                                              Oh, Sir!
I stand by the gate. I am a friend of the family.
Pray read this tract before it is too late!

Variations on a Street Song

Ten little girls from school are we,
plaited, pony-tailed, socks to the knee.
Some are as smart as smart can be,
and each one of us is pretty.

Rosie Fagan says she'll cry
if she doesn't get the fellow with the roving eye.
Elsie Geraghty says she'll die
for want of the Golden City.

The wind, the wind, the wind blows high
the rain comes tumbling from the sky

Some are bound to travel far,
go through the world like a shooting star.
Some will shunt like an old street car.

Some will fall right over the edge
to the place where all the nightmares lodge.
Some will always cling to a ledge.

The wind, the wind, the wind blows high
the snow comes drifting from the sky

Some get pudding and still want pie.
Some settle for a fellow with a roving eye,
and some will pine and some will die
for want of the Golden City.

Mrs. Pintrap

met on a cold day
skewered me with her eye

why?

I was looking too happy
perhaps

clearly an expert
one glance did it

my appearance
eccentric
accessories
frivolous
tentative smile
dismissed

Mrs. Pintrap
though your scalpel eye
fillet me, flesh
from bone

I will stand here
in my backbone and ribcage
and say

God loves you too
Mrs. Pintrap

Old Wives' Tales

Prompt at the equinox came the gales.
(Such things were old wives' tales, he'd told her.)
The windows streamed, the trees bent over.

Being a man, he'd had things to do.
Being a woman, she'd watched weather.

Oh listen, you who can quarry caverns
and pile your towers as steep as heaven,
for we can tell where the wind will come from
to scatter them all and send them flying.

Herald of Spring

There I was in bed with a cold, when Mr. McGinty
(he said his name was McGinty) came to the door
and offered to prune the cherry and the laburnum
for twelve pounds. 'What do you think?' said John.
'It ought to be done,' said I, 'and I don't want you
risking your neck up a tree.'

                    So Mr. McGinty
got the OK, and I must have dozed, for I wakened
and turned over, and there was Mr. McGinty,
framed in the half-drawn curtains, up the tree,
his hat on his head, his overcoat tails flapping,
smoking a cigarette.

                    I was sorry I'd seen it.
No visiting wrens and finches have blurred that image
of Mr. McGinty perched like a giant crow
in the thin bending branches.

                    'He says he's left us
ready for spring. There should be masses of blossom,'
said John to me, and I said 'All's well if it ends well,'

but a stranger handmaiden of Flora I never did see
than Mr. McGinty sitting smoking in our tree.

Camel Bells

Camel bells in a cluster
dangle beside the door
of your room, and the silken rope
hangs down as far as the hall.
I used to tug it, and hope
that the tinkling sound would reach
through whatever music you played
or whatever Shakespearean speech
you declaimed.

                There is no one to call
now. I go up to your room.
The dolls' house behind the door,
the ballet shoes, and the blue
Picasso are waiting. I finger
the books – Rabbit Hill, beside Pinter
and Sartre. Pale on the floor
lingers the cold sun of winter.
There is nobody here.

                      I brush
past the bells on the landing. The sound
tinkles as faint as a ghost
and loud as a wave that I drown in.

Coming Alive

The room imposes silence.   Visitors drift,
alone or whispering, past these relics, dug
from the dark, exposed, behind rectangular glass,
in the stark light of today.

Saddle-cloths and bridles.   Worked gold,
carved bone.   Skin of an arm
preserved for the tattoo.   The air shivers
with distant sounds.

Hacked-off head of a warrior.   Woman's shoe,
extravagantly embroidered.   Coat of a child,
aged two, perhaps, or three,

                            who is here
all of a sudden, the wind whipping
fur of his collar against a round cheek,
slant eyes impassive, watching
jostling ponies and men.

                            Then he is gone
again, scurrying off, intent
on his own affairs, vanishing
into the future, without his coat.
I hear him along the carpeted corridor
and down the steps.   A wind from the High Altai
fumbles the dry leaves of an early winter
in Bloomsbury Square.

Apparition in W. H. Smith's

came through the door
just like a person, but no
person to see, only
thin black pillar, dull
black hanging in folds, shiny
black in folds where face
ought to be, feet walking, bringing
what? – waveringly came, aslant,
like hollow ghost, like hooded dead

              like gaping nothing
underfoot where ground
ought to be

              backward look
tracks her, black-
veiled Arab lady queuing at the
photograph counter

Photographs?

Of what?

Instructions for a Funeral

The car will come. You will hear it.
The bell will ring.   Stand up.
Go to the door.

It will do you no good
not to go.

The music you are prepared for.
But words find chinks.   Be careful.

Then down the path, one foot
before the other.   You are not given
a choice.

Then thud of earth on wood.
You will recognise it.

Go home then, one foot
before the other.   Shut
the door.

Then turn and look at
the rest of your life.

Schoolgirls Crossing the Park

In harsh light of early
March they dawdle, in a
shrill wind, scuffing
gravel, hair all spikes
and anyhow, fists bunched
in duffle pockets, knees
and elbows gawky as twigs

past delved municipal
beds prodded
from sleep by blunt
stabs of crocus.

             Soon
sap and blood will run
more smooth and singing.
Mild sun will gentle
awkward limbs to leaves,
to pliant flesh, to birdsong
and eyeshine.